Thankyou Dad & Mum for nurturing my creativity. And Chris... I just love you! ♡♥And Dear Laura!♡

For my son

James ♥ ♡ ♡ ♡

In memory of Auntie Celia, Grandma Eva, Lovely Renée,

♡ ♡ In memory of "A thankful life is a happy life". Thankyou Jared-my love-for your faithful Love and support.!!

Amelia is a very rare fish, a very rare fish indeed. She is the colour of golden sunshine, and on her tail are hairs, green like the grass.

She moves gently in the water, like a ballerina moving in step to a harmony.

Amelia is an inquisitive fish. She loves to explore. As she swims through the ocean she wiggles her fins in delight at every new discovery, friend and treasure.

When she laughs,
little bubbles come
out of her mouth and
soar upwards through
the water.

She often finds hidden things under rocks at the bottom of the ocean. She finds gold and gemstones and treasures that had been lost for a long time.

A few of the fish near Amelia think that she is too unusual and different from them, as she is the only fish with bubbles on her body.

"grumpus muchus" - a very grumpy fish -

With sheer terror screeching from their mouths they speak awful lies to Amelia, and she begins to believe them. Amelia feels deeply in her heart that she must hide, and she dives into the nearest patch of seaweed and buries herself there.

A long time seems to pass as Amelia rests comfortably in the tall green swaying leaves of the sea-weed. Then one day she glimpses a strange and unusual sight far off in the distance. Amelia sees a shimmering city of light.

Amelia's
heart has an awakening
and begins
to stir deep
inside of her.

A longing to explore the ocean fills her heart again, and it sounds like a marching band playing a triumphant melody.

Amelia's eyes begin to brighten, and a smile creeps across her face. Hope fills her heart, and curiosity bubbles up inside of her like a fountain.

Inside of Amelia's heart courage is exploding, and it is as refreshing to her as drinking cold water on a hot day.

All of a sudden, she knows that she cannot hide inside the seaweed anymore, and she pushes her way out, venturing back into the vast ocean.

She sets her gaze upon the city of light, and firmly decides that this will be her new destination.

Soon Amelia arrives at the city of light and peeks one open  inside of the windows. Light is bursting forth in every direction and dazzles her eyes.

The flickering colours of light are so magnificent that they almost scare her, but so beautiful that she cannot take her eyes off of them. Her golden scales are lit up, and Amelia now has colours more radiant than have ever been seen on a fish BEFORE!

Amelia could contain her joy no longer. She firmly decided to swim back and find the other fish to introduce them to the light. She knew that she must also go to the ones that teased her, for surely they needed it the most.

Upon her arrival, the other fish were amazed to see how she had changed. She was beautiful and magnificent to all eyes that beheld her.

Never before had they seen a fish so wonderfully radiant. They were delighted, and became intrigued to experience this light for themselves.

one by one, all of the fish swam towards the city of light, and they were transformed. Each fish had the same explosion of joy and hope in their hearts. Every fish shone brightly with beautiful dazzling colours.

So all of the fish, luminous as they were, spread across the ocean deep to find new friends who had never seen the city of light.

Now the depths of the ocean, which had been a dark, dark place, shone brightly with fish more magnificent and glorious than perhaps you have ever seen before.

And do you know what happened?

Before very long, the entire ocean glowed and radiated with the colours of the fish and the world never looked the same again!

"muchus joyus"
- a very happy fish-

www.stephaniebalke.org
contact@stephaniebalke.org

www.ingramcontent.com/pod-product-compliance
Lightning Source LLC
Chambersburg PA
CBHW041544240626
47164CB00002B/127